In memory of my parents and their own plastic choirboy, bought with Top Value trading stamps many years ago. He was the only outdoor Christmas decoration they ever owned, and has inspired this story. One windy night shortly before Christmas, a strong gust picked him up and hurled him high in the air. . . .

SIMON & SCHUSTER BOOKS FOR YOUNG READERS • An imprint of Simon & Schuster Children's Publishing Division • 1230 Avenue of the Americas, New York, New York 10020 • Copyright © 2016 by Scott Santoro • All rights reserved, including the right of reproduction in whole or in part in any form. • SIMON & SCHUSTER BOOKS FOR YOUNG READERS is a trademark of Simon & Schuster, Inc. • For information about special discounts for bulk purchases, please contact Simon & Schuster Special Sales at 1-866-506-1949 or business@simonandschuster.com. • The Simon & Schuster Speakers Bureau can bring authors to your live event. For more information or to book an event, contact the Simon & Schuster Speakers Bureau at 1-866-248-3049 or visit our website at www.simonspeakers.com. • Book design by Laurent Linn • The text for this book was set in Nueva Std. • The illustrations for this book were rendered digitally. • Manufactured in China • 0716 SCP • First Edition • 10 9 8 7 6 5 4 3 2 1 • Library of Congress Cataloging-in-Publication Data • Names: Santoro, Scott, author. • Title: Candy Cane Lane / Scott Santoro. • Description: 1st edition. | New York : Simon & Schuster Books for Young Readers, [2016] | Identifiers: LCCN 2015044733 | ISBN 9781481456616 (hardback) | ISBN 9781481456623 (eBook) • Subjects: | CYAC: Christmas decorations—Fiction. | Christmas—Fiction. | BISAC: JUVENILE FICTION / Holidays & Celebrations / Christmas & Advent. | JUVENILE FICTION / Action & Adventure / General. | JUVENILE FICTION / Humorous Stories. | Classification: LCC PZ7.S23855 Can 2016 | DDC [E]—dc23 LC record available at https://lccn.loc.gov/2015044733

# CANDY CANE LANE

Scott Santoro

SIMON & SCHUSTER BOOKS FOR YOUNG READERS
NEW YORK  LONDON  TORONTO  SYDNEY  NEW DELHI

Every year at Christmas, people would come from miles around to see the famous decorations on Candy Cane Lane. There were twenty-eight snowmen, fifteen wise men, thirty-eight Santas, seventy-two reindeer, an army of tin soldiers, and many, many others.

But there was also a plain house at the end of the lane. The little girl who lived inside knew her father could not afford fancy lawn ornaments.

Sometimes, when the lights were most magical, she wished that they could have just one figure for their little lawn.

A few nights before Christmas,
a blizzard hit Candy Cane Lane.

The next morning, ornaments were scattered across lawns and rooftops.

The little girl gasped! A little plastic choirboy, dented and
scuffed from his fall, had been stuffed into a trash bin.
*How wonderful he would look on our lawn,* she thought.
She rescued him and hurried back to her house.

But later that day, her father assumed the choirboy had been blown
from the trash by the wind, so he stuffed him back into the bin.
A garbage truck snatched him up.

And as it roared and bounced away, the choirboy
watched Candy Cane Lane fade from sight.

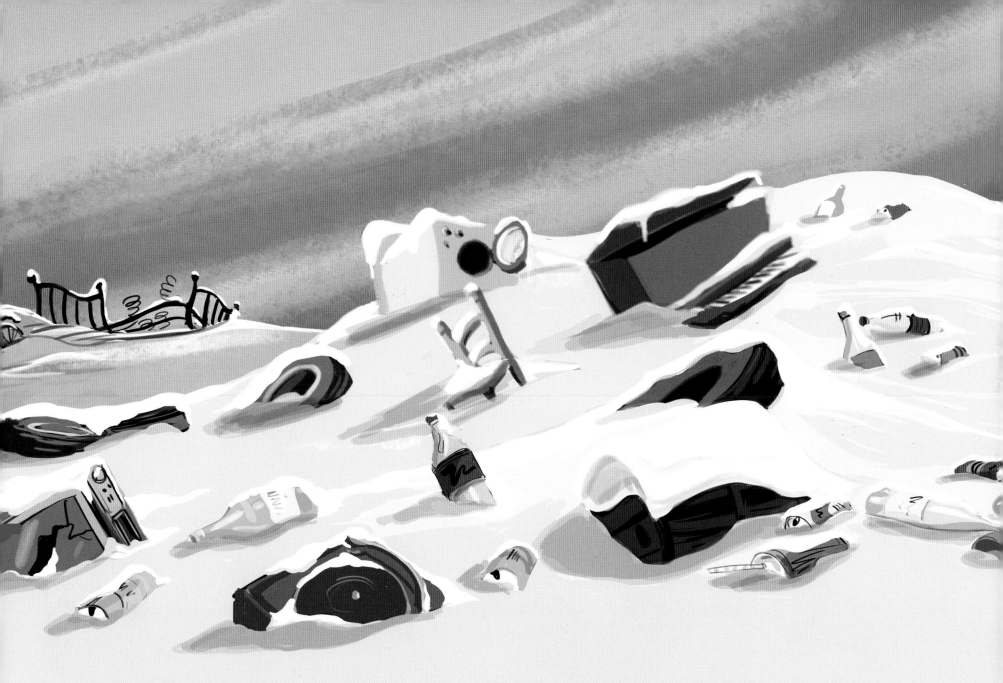

After many hours, the garbage truck stopped and tipped its load,
and the choirboy rolled down a large pile of garbage. Here there
were no twinkling lights, no Christmas carols, no Candy Cane Lane.

"Wonderful storm, wasn't it?" A broken reindeer leapt onto a nearby pile of garbage. "Wind blew me straight off the roof! Sure, I lost an antler, but I finally know what it feels like to fly!"

"Where are we?" asked the choirboy.

"For things like us, it's the end of the line,"
said a hollow voice nearby.

"A ghost!" the choirboy sang out in fright.

"Not a real ghost," the ghost said with a laugh. "But thank you very much." The choirboy told them about the girl who'd tried to save him. "We need to find our way back to Candy Cane Lane," he said.

So together they set off on foot toward the bright lights in the distance.

But those lights turned out to be a busy shopping center surrounded by busier roads. "The world is a much bigger place than I supposed," said the choirboy.

The three new friends walked a very long way. They walked past superhighways.

They walked through woods and fields.

They walked past giant factories. "Oh, it's no use," said the choirboy. "This doesn't look anything like beautiful Candy Cane Lane."

"What on earth is that!" exclaimed the reindeer.
It was a giant, standing on the roof of a factory. The giant chuckled in a deep, booming voice. "Welcome! You look as though you have entertained many, many people over the years."

Standing in the doorway was the most beautiful sugarplum fairy the choirboy had ever seen.

"Have you journeyed far?" she asked. "You must tell me about the outside world. You see, I've never left the factory. They keep me here on permanent display."

They followed her to the assembly line, where two hundred Santas waited to be painted.

"Spooky! They're all identical!" gasped the ghost.

"Actually, not all of them," said the sugarplum fairy. She led them to the next room. . . .

There they found dozens of ornaments who looked very different.
There was a Santa with a green coat, a camel with three humps,
wise men without gifts, and a snowman who looked melted.

"They were all rejected," the sugarplum fairy said in a low voice.

"You must all come home with me to Candy Cane Lane," said the choirboy. "There's a little girl there who would love to have us all."

"Hooray!" shouted the others.

"There's just one problem. I'm afraid I don't know the way."

"Perhaps I can help," suggested the giant.
"I can carry all of you in my great arms."

Along the way they passed several busy highways,
but Candy Cane Lane was nowhere in sight.

"There's an elf!" cried the choirboy. "Perhaps he knows where Candy Cane Lane is."

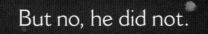

But no, he did not.

Neither did Burger Kid or Little Cupcake.
"I'm afraid we're never going to find Candy Cane Lane," said the ghost.
"If I were a *real* flying reindeer, I could fly high enough to spot Candy Cane Lane," said the reindeer.

"Maybe you *can* be a real flying reindeer!" exclaimed the choirboy. "Mr. Giant, you must throw us as high as you possibly can."

An updraft took them higher and higher until they could see the whole city.
"There it is!" shouted the choirboy. "There's Candy Cane Lane!"

The reindeer landed on the little girl's rooftop
as lightly as any flying reindeer ever did.

The giant helped deliver the rest of the ornaments safely, and in the pink light of dawn he hurried back to the factory before he was missed.

The little girl woke up because she thought she heard singing.

"You did this while I was sleeping, didn't you, Dad?
And you even brought back the choirboy!"

"This is the most wonderful Christmas I could ever imagine!" exclaimed the little girl.

And all the ornaments agreed.